MICHAEL DAHL'S
REALLY SCARY STORIES

Michael Dahl's Really Scary Stories
are published by Stone Arch Books,
A Capstone Imprint
1710 Roe Crest Drive
North Mankato, Minnesota 56003
www.capstonepub.com

Library of Congress Cataloging-in-Publication Data
Dahl, Michael, author.
   The phantom on the phone and other scary tales / by Michael Dahl
; illustrated by Xavier Bonet.
        pages cm. -- (Michael Dahl's Really scary stories))
   Summary: One morning Ella gets an odd text message from a friend,
about a strange girl who is showing up in Ella's selfies, and as
the messages keep coming the girl with a monkey head keeps getting
closer and closer — and that is only one of the chilling tales in
this collection of scary stories.
   ISBN 978-1-4965-0597-2 (library binding) -- ISBN 978-1-4965-2335-8
(ebook pdf)
1. Horror tales, American. 2. Children's stories, American. [1. Horror
stories. 2. Short stories.] I. Bonet, Xavier, 1979- illustrator. II.
Title.
   PZ7.D15134Ph 2015
   813.54--dc23
   [Fic]

                                    2015001877

Designer: Hilary Wacholz
Image Credits: Dmitry Natashin

Printed in the United States of America.
009452R

THE PHANTOM
ON THE PHONE
AND OTHER SCARY TALES

By Michael Dahl

Illustrated by
Xavier Bonet

STONE ARCH BOOKS
a capstone imprint

TABLE OF
CONTENTS

The shadowy figure wearing the bag shifted back and forth on his feet. He seemed impatient, wanting to move.

Jordan picked one up for a closer look. Startled, he dropped the box on the grass. They weren't pieces of chalk.

The fingers moved. Both boys jumped back. In the fresh hole that Jeremy had dug, the dirt was stirring.

Dear Reader,

When I was ten years old, I read a book called *Eight Tales of Terror*.

This book was written by Edgar Allan Poe, a famous author who created frightening and mysterious stories.

My house was empty when I got home. I sat down to read the book in a high-backed chair in the living room. It was the middle of a spring afternoon, with cheerful sunlight streaming through the windows.

As I turned each page, I kept looking up, glancing behind me, listening for unusual sounds.

I WAS TERRIFIED.

That night I read all eight of the stories again.

Now it is your turn to read. Seven tales of terror await you.

BE BRAVE.

Michael Dahl

HALLOWEEN
HEAD

Oliver stood on the dark lawn while laughter and movement and flashing cell phones whirled around him. Throngs of kids were walking up and down the sidewalks, crossing the streets, laughing and talking cheerfully. They lifted their masks to talk to each other. They bent their heads to check out the goodies in each other's trick-or-treat bags. A few of the more eager kids sucked on lollipops or chewed on chocolate bars.

Oliver stood quietly, without moving a muscle. He was staring at something, or rather someone, at the end of the street.

A kid in a fat bumblebee costume ran up to him. "Ollie! Look at the score from the

Hansons' house! They give you three different candy bars!"

Normally this kind of news would make Oliver's eyes pop and his saliva glands go into overdrive. But Oliver didn't move. He held up a finger to silence his friend. "Joseph," he said quietly. "Take a look down the street."

Joseph looked. Then he shrugged. "So? It's just some kid."

"But who is he?" said Oliver.

"Some big teenager who wants candy," said Joseph. "That must be why he's only wearing a mask. He's too cool."

Weird mask, thought Oliver. The tall teenager, wearing a T-shirt, a jacket, and jeans, was also wearing a paper grocery bag over his head with two small slits for eyeholes.

"But I haven't seen him go up to any house," said Oliver. "And he's not carrying a bag for candy."

Joseph clutched his own bag more tightly to his bumblebee body. "Do you think he steals candy from other people? He's not getting

11

mine! No way!" Then he sprinted off the lawn and down the sidewalk, away from the masked teenager.

He's not getting mine either, thought Oliver. *Candy is my life.* Halloween was the only time of year when Oliver could get mountains of candy absolutely free. He wasn't going to let this night go to waste.

The shadowy figure wearing the bag shifted back and forth on his feet. He seemed impatient, wanting to move.

Oliver had three or four more blocks to hit before he headed home. Then he'd be in his own bedroom and wouldn't have to think about the weird kid wearing the bag. But after the next house, Oliver noticed the teenager standing under the streetlight across the street. Then after the second house, he saw him standing in the yard next door. And after the third house, when Oliver's bag was growing almost too heavy with its sugary loot, the teen stood on the sidewalk just in front of the house next-door.

The masked figure was waiting.

Oliver thought of copying his bumblebee pal, Joseph, and running toward home, dashing through his neighbors' front yards. But instead, he grew angry. He was afraid of this stranger following him, and the fear made him mad. *Who is this guy anyway?* Oliver wondered. *Why is he following me? There's no way I'm giving up my candy.*

A full moon hung in the dark October sky, white as a marshmallow. It was very late, and most trick-or-treaters had gone home. Oliver could hear voices a few blocks away. The faint sound of closing doors. Dying laughter and screams.

There was no one else on the block but him and the masked teen. If the older kid tried to grab Oliver's bag or knock him down and run, there was nobody around to witness it or run after the thief. He could always scream, but Oliver felt that screaming was for wimps.

Oliver hoisted up his bag, walked down the sidewalk, and headed toward his shadowy stalker.

He stopped a few feet away from the teen. His legs felt like they were made of licorice, but

he stood up tall. "What's the big deal?" Oliver asked angrily. "Why do you keep following me?"

The grocery bag tilted down toward Oliver. But the teen did not answer.

"Who are you?" asked Oliver. The tiny slits stared at him, but the teen still didn't make a sound. "Can't you talk?"

The masked figure slowly swayed back and forth, shifting his weight from one foot to the other. He didn't make any move toward Oliver. He simply stared.

"Just leave me alone," said Oliver. He held onto his bag with both hands and started walking past the teen. The teen did not back out of the way in time. Oliver brushed against his jacket. He braced himself, expecting a hand to dart out and shove him to the sidewalk, but nothing happened.

Oliver turned around quickly. Anger boiled up inside of him. And then, without thinking or planning, Oliver reached up and snatched at the paper bag. "Who are you?!"

Oliver heard a high-pitched scream. Then he realized it was coming from his own wide-

open mouth. With the paper bag in his hand, he stared at the teen and saw there was no head on his shoulders. Not even a neck.

The figure started to wave his arms around blindly, searching for his bag with the slits for eyeholes. He stumbled off the sidewalk and onto the street.

Suddenly, there was another high-pitched sound. Squealing brakes. The headless figure fell in front of a car and smashed onto the road. Oliver watched, frozen with fear. He watched as the teen's body seemed to crumple like paper. His skin rippled open, like a popped balloon, spilling a thousand pieces of candy onto the asphalt, glittering in the car's headlights. Red and pink and white, like blood and skin and bones.

The man driving the car and the woman in the passenger's seat jumped out. "What happened?" he yelled.

"You hit someone! You hit someone!" the woman shrieked.

The man shook his head, staring at the mass of candy gleaming in the headlights.

"Hey, kid!" he shouted to Oliver. "You saw what happened, right?"

Oliver got out of there fast. He ran through the dark spaces under the trees and stumbled across his neighbors' yards. His eyes were glazed. His hand was glued to his bag.

After a few blocks, his feet hit a sidewalk. He blinked and saw that he was close to his house. On this block, a few kids were still running up to houses, pressing doorbells and yelling for treats.

A kid in a werewolf costume started to walk past Oliver, but Oliver stopped him. "Hey," he said. "Do you like candy?"

"Who doesn't?" said the werewolf.

Oliver handed him his candy bag. "Take it," he said. "I don't eat the stuff anymore."

Then Oliver turned and walked toward his house, without realizing he was still tightly clutching the other bag, the one with slits for eyeholes. And the slits were staring at his head.

CHALK

A huge, gross monster with bloody fangs and seven horns took up the entire driveway.

Jordan was returning from a bike ride with his friends. When he turned into the driveway, he saw the monster and braked. His younger sister, Nyla, was on her hands and knees, resting on the creature's belly. The belly, like every other part of the creature, was bone white. Nyla was finishing the last row of scales when she heard Jordan behind her.

"What is all this?" Jordan asked.

Nyla looked up. A skinny white object rested in her hand.

"It's my pet dragon," she said.

"Are you nuts? Dad said no drawing on the driveway," Jordan said.

Nyla shrugged and returned to drawing. "Daddy will think my dragon is beautiful," she said.

"Daddy will ground you and send you to your room," said Jordan. Their father was an architect and worked from home. When people visited him during the day, he wanted to impress them with their beautiful house that he had designed. A messy driveway was a bad first impression.

Nyla kept drawing.

Jordan had to admit that the dragon looked awesome. He didn't know Nyla was such a good artist. It must have taken her hours to draw that dragon. It was full of details like the blood dripping from its teeth, the sharp lines of its three white eyes, and a curling tail with hundreds of scales. The whole drawing must have been fifteen feet long.

"How long have you been out here?" Jordan asked.

"A few minutes," Nyla said.

"You're lying," Jordan said.

"Am not!" cried Nyla.

"Nobody could draw all this in a few minutes," Jordan pointed out.

"But I did!" said Nyla, frowning at him. "The poor lady said it was special chalk."

"What lady?" asked Jordan.

Nyla held up a small wooden box. "She gave me this."

Jordan dropped his bike on the grass and walked over to grab the box.

"She said I could draw pretty things with the chalk," Nyla said.

The red wooden box felt light in Jordan's hands. He saw that there were tiny drawings carved into the wood. There were sharp brass thingies at the corners that poked his hands.

"The poor lady walked away, and then you came," said Nyla.

Jordan opened the box.

"The poor lady said it was a present," said Nyla.

In the bottom of the box lay four long pieces of chalk. They looked like the one Nyla was using. Jordan picked one up for a closer look. Startled, he dropped the box and the piece of chalk on the grass. But they weren't pieces of chalk. They were fingers. Skeleton fingers.

Nyla smiled at her dragon.

"The poor lady was so nice," said Nyla.

Jordan could hardly breathe. "Why do you keep calling her 'the poor lady'?"

"I feel sorry for her," said Nyla as she kept drawing. "She only had one hand."

NIGHT CRAWLERS

Two boys on bikes appeared from a line of trees by a lonely lake. They braked a few feet from the water's edge.

"I don't hear anything," whispered Sean, the first boy.

"No one lives around here," said the other boy, Jeremy. "Nice and quiet."

The lake was an almost perfect circle, surrounded by a wide shore and a thick band of trees. The still water reflected the sky above, making the lake look like a vast blue hole. A hole as endless as space.

Sean watched a few white clouds drift across the water's surface.

"Does your brother still fish here?" Sean asked.

Jeremy shook his head. "He never fished here. He just heard about it from some guy at school. I don't think many people come here. No real roads lead here — just the trail."

The boys got off their bikes and slid their heavy backpacks onto the ground. They set up the tent, rolled out their sleeping bags, and organized their gear. They were unpacking their fishing rods when Sean noticed a dark, low shape on the lake. He thought it was moving. The boys continued to unpack their supplies but kept an eye on the shape. It grew larger as it neared the shore. Both boys jumped up and ran toward the water.

It was a small, gray rowboat. Large enough for two passengers, but no one was inside.

"The oars are still inside," said Jeremy.

"How did it get here?" said Sean. "There's no wind."

"It drifted," said Jeremy. He waded out a few feet and grabbed a rope at the front of the boat. He and Sean and dragged it onto the shore.

Jeremy frowned. "You think someone fell out and drowned?" he asked.

"We didn't hear anything," said Sean.

Jeremy cupped his hands to his mouth and shouted. His echo rang loudly through the forest, across the lake and back again. There was no reply. "If someone was yelling before we got here, we would have heard it out on the trail," said Jeremy.

"Dead man's boat," Sean muttered to himself.

Jeremy swatted at a mosquito. "Don't get weird," he said. "It's old. It's probably been out here a long time. We can't do anything now, anyway. We're all set up."

Sean slowly nodded and rubbed his arms. The air was getting cooler, and the sun was lower in the sky. *We may as well stay and have some fun,* he thought.

It was too late to start fishing, so the boys built a small fire and cooked hot dogs and pizza rolls for dinner. Shadows deepened around their tent as they drank sodas and ate candy bars. When the sun had almost set and the sky was turning the color of cheddar cheese,

Jeremy grabbed a flashlight. "Now's the fun part," he said.

"Night crawlers!" they both yelled.

Sean grabbed his own flashlight and an empty bucket. Carrying shovels and swinging their beams from side to side, they carefully made their way into the woods. The boys considered night crawlers, or earthworms, the best bait around. Digging up the worms themselves, instead of paying for them at a bait shop, always made them feel like true outdoorsmen. Tonight they'd hunt for night crawlers and use them to fish in the lake.

Jeremy stopped and stamped on the moist earth. He set his foot on the shovel and pushed down with all his weight. Sean did the same.

"The worms are supposed to be nice and fat here," said Jeremy, puffing a little as he dug. "They don't call this place Night Crawler Lake for nothing."

"You said this lake didn't have a name," said Sean.

Jeremy shrugged, but kept turning over the rich, black soil. "That's just a nickname."

With their flashlights, the boys scanned the dirt. Dozens of pinkish worms, thick as fingers, squirmed and wriggled.

"What did I tell ya?" said Jeremy. He scooped up handfuls of worms and dropped them in the bucket. He nodded. "Nice," he said.

It wasn't long before the bucket was overflowing with thick, juicy night crawlers.

"You were right about this place," said Sean.

"C'mon, let's get some more," said Jeremy, heading farther into the woods.

"We've got plenty," said Sean.

Jeremy ignored him. "I want a few more," he said, and he kept walking.

Sean followed, but he wasn't happy about it. Soon, he heard Jeremy exclaim, "These are the best! Look, Sean. Look how big they are."

Sean had to admit the new worms lying at his friend's feet were huge — pink, wet sausages.

Jeremy bent over to pick them up. He quickly dropped them with a shout. He pointed with his shaking flashlight. "Not . . . not worms . . ."

It was a man's hand. Chopped off neatly at the wrist.

"My — my shovel must have cut it off," Jeremy said.

Sean felt sick to his stomach. "But what's it doing out —"

The fingers moved. Both boys jumped back. In the fresh hole that Jeremy had dug, the dirt was stirring. A second hand, this one attached to a muddy arm, reached up from the ground.

The boys dropped their shovels and flashlights and darted behind a tree trunk. The arm was followed by a shoulder and then a man's head. Then his entire torso. Silently, the man pulled himself free from the ground. He raised himself to all fours and crawled slowly across the ground, his head moving from side to side as if he was searching for something. Heavy, wet earth dripped from his body.

The forest filled with rustling sounds. As their eyes adjusted to the dark, Sean and Jeremy could faintly see another shape moving along the ground about twenty feet away. A second man crawling slowly along the forest floor.

Jeremy gripped his shoulder. "Look over there," he said.

Another figure was struggling out of the ground behind the first two. Leaves and twigs rustled as the crawlers moved over them. Sean counted seven more figures digging their way out of the damp soil. He thought one or two might be women, because of their long hair hanging down, hair that was streaked with mud and leaves.

Something rustled at their feet. The boys turned and saw two hands reaching up through the dirt. Five more shadows gathered a few yards away. All the shadows were crawling toward them.

The boys didn't care if they made any noise as they fled back toward the lake. They saw more and more people crawling among the trees, moving silently toward them.

"I told you we had enough worms!" yelled Sean. "You should have stopped."

Jeremy cupped his hands to his mouth and shouted for help. His echo died in the empty air.

Crash!

Several of the crawlers had plowed through the boys' tent, knocking over their bikes and their supplies. The crawlers moved as if in a trance, not caring what stood in their way. There were dozens of them, caked in mud. Rotting clothes hung in tatters from their stiff bodies. The boys kept backing up, until they felt the lake water at their ankles.

"The boat," said Jeremy.

They jumped into the rowboat, grabbed the oars, and began rowing away from the shore.

"We should be safe out here, right?" Jeremy asked, breathing hard.

Twenty or more crawlers had stopped at the lake's edge, sniffing at the water. Then they pushed ahead. The creatures splashed into the lake and soon disappeared underwater. Once the first line of crawlers slid under, another came close behind. It seemed the forest would never run out of them. Like a swarm of oversized army ants, the creatures crawled into the lake.

Jeremy and Sean rowed farther away. In his panic, Jeremy lost hold of his oar and

dropped it in the water. Instead of floating, as it should have done, the oar quickly sank out of sight. Sean tried to row even harder with the remaining oar, but he only succeeded in making them turn in circles.

"Wait," said Jeremy. "They're gone."

The shore was empty. Nothing moved under the trees. The lake was silent and peaceful.

"Let's go back," said Jeremy. "We'll get our bikes and go."

Goose bumps ran up and down Sean's bare arms. "There's something wrong," he said. He gazed over the edge of the rowboat. The rippling water was black as oil. The boat gently bobbed up and down like an Adam's apple in a swallowing throat.

"No, no," said Sean. "This is all wrong."

"What are you talking about?" said Jeremy.

"There are no bubbles," said Sean.

"So?"

"No one's breathing," said Sean. "They don't need air!"

Before Jeremy could respond, Sean's oar was ripped from his grasp. The boat rocked as if hundreds of hands were pushing and shoving and guiding the boat farther and farther from shore. The boys didn't shout for help. They knew no one would hear them. After all, they hadn't heard anyone yelling when they'd arrived at the lake.

By the time the moon rose above the trees, the boat was empty. The lake was quiet. But under the oily waves, shadows squirmed and wriggled, like a thousand hungry night crawlers.

THE WORLD'S MOST AWESOME TOOTHPASTE

Jared was not a morning person, but his little brother, Harry, was. Every morning, as the two of them got ready for school, he could hear Harry sing out from his bedroom down the hall:

Morning glory,

Morning lark,

Evening owl

Dim and dark.

This morning, Harry was screeching at the top of his tiny lungs. Jared stuck his fingers in his ears and trudged toward the bathroom. He gazed into the mirror above the sink, trying to

focus, but he could barely open his eyes. His hair stuck up like angry feathers.

He turned on the cold water and felt around in the medicine cabinet for the tube of toothpaste. Brushing teeth was his Number Two most un-favorite thing in the world. Number One was waking up.

The toothpaste tube felt strangely full and solid. Jared looked down and saw that it was new. A brand he'd never seen before. He squinted at the bright red and golden letters. THE WORLD'S MOST AWESOME TOOTHPASTE.

It was probably cheaper than the regular brand, and his mom was always trying to save a few more cents.

Jared squeezed some glowing white paste onto the stiff bristles of his toothbrush. He raised the brush and stuck it in his mouth. His eyes popped open.

Wow! The taste was amazing. It was like nothing he'd ever tasted before. No, it was like *everything* he'd ever tasted before. He felt as if he'd just drunk ten sodas in a second. Twenty.

Zing! Energy pulsed through his body. *Zang!* Lightning bolted through his brain cells.

This *was* the world's most awesome toothpaste.

Jared couldn't stop himself. It was just too good. He kept brushing. The awesomeness kept growing and growing. The toothpaste kept glowing and glowing.

He ignored the big green clock hanging over the toilet. Who cared if he missed the bus? Big deal if he was late for his first-period art class.

Tink!

Jared looked down. One of his teeth had landed in the metal sink. No big deal. It must have been loose anyway. Jared spit out some of the toothpaste, added more to his bristles, and then continued brushing. He noticed that the water in the sink was turning pink. But it didn't stop him. Jared shrugged, closed his eyes, and kept brushing.

He had to. It was awesome!

The bathroom door swung open.

His brother's little blond head edged around

the door and he said, "Come on, Jared. You're making us late —"

Harry froze. Then he screamed. And kept screaming.

Jared stared at him. He looked in the mirror again.

Half of his face was missing. He had brushed away the skin until it was shiny, white bone. The sink was full of blood. His tongue was in tatters.

But his smile? It was awesome!

THE BACK OF THE CLOSET

I wake up. It's very dark. Everyone should be in bed by now, but I can hear footsteps. They're by the closet.

Creeeeeak!

I can see the closet door opening. I'm too startled to speak. Am I dreaming? I must be dreaming, because now I see a skinny, hairless hand.

The hand opens its fingers as it reaches.

The hand pulls the cord hanging from the closet ceiling, and the light snaps on.

It's so bright!

The hand definitely belongs to one of the small humans that live in this house. None of them have seen me hiding in this closet. They don't realize that I've been here a very long time. Ever since the house was built.

No one has ever bothered to look at the very back of this closet. Lucky for me. It's in the basement of the house, and hardly any of the humans come to this particular corner. The shadows here are quite comfy.

I hope the young human doesn't see me hiding here behind these boxes. What is it looking for anyway? There's nothing in here but old, broken things.

Ah, it's reaching for an old toy. Lots of toys were left here by another family. The small human must be looking for something to do.

I decide I don't want the small human coming here to my home, so I make a noise, reach out, and spook it. And now, I'm sure it'll stay away.

Forever.

THE ELF'S
LAST TRICK

Nathan heard the scream and smiled. *This is the best prank ever,* he thought.

He had come up with the plan only the day before. It began when his teacher, Mr. Garcia, returned the students' book reports before the final bell. Mr. Garcia weaved in and out of the rows, dropping a report on each desk. At the top of Nathan's report was a C minus scrawled in red, bright as a bug bite. *A C minus?* Nathan thought. *Well, I* did *write the report in less than twenty minutes, and most of it I copied off the Internet. So what? It still doesn't deserve such a low grade. Teachers are so unfair.*

At the bottom of his report was a note from Mr. Garcia. "Nathan, you can do so much better than

this!" Nathan hated when teachers said that. How did they know what he could or couldn't do?

He crumpled up the paper and shoved it in his desk. He hoped no one nearby saw the horrible red grade. Nathan was sure his face was red, too. He looked at Mr. Garcia and glared. What a fake smile the teacher had. *Fake smile.* That's when Nathan remembered the elf. And that's when the plan began forming in his brain.

Nathan's family loved to play pranks. Even the grown-ups got into it. Last winter, Nathan's mom had bought an elf doll as a Christmas decoration. Its thick, puffy body was two feet high, with bendable legs and arms. The oversized head had lobster-red hair tucked under an emerald green cap with a white puffball on top. The face looked real. Hard, bright eyes, rosy cheeks, a wide smile with teeth. Everyone agreed that the doll looked creepy. Which made it perfect for scary tricks.

The first victim had been Nathan. Nathan's dad had hid the elf in his bed. After the boy had gone up to his room, his scream echoed through the house. It was followed by hoots of laughter. The elf showed up more and more in the coming months. More screams. More laughs. More and more pranks. Finally, when the family had grown

tired of the elf, and no one jumped or gasped when they saw its eerie smile coming from a closet or refrigerator or washing machine, the creature was stuffed in a box, along with the other holiday decorations, stacked on a shelf in the garage, and forgotten.

But Nathan remembered. Coming home from school, still angry about the unfair grade, he went straight to the garage. He climbed onto a chair, pulled the box from its shelf, snuck the elf into his bedroom, and stuffed it in his backpack. The next day, he walked to school extra early and hid the elf in his locker.

When the last bell rang, Nathan stayed after school in the media center. After a while, he quietly slipped out of the center and hurried to his locker. He stuffed the elf into his backpack again, looking around to make sure no one saw him, and raced down the empty halls toward Mr. Garcia's room.

The door was unlocked. Nathan crept over to Mr. Garcia's desk. He placed the elf on the teacher's chair, and then turned it so the elf was facing away. When Mr. Garcia came in the next morning, he would turn his chair back around and — surprise! The elf would strike again.

Nathan had just stepped outside and closed the door when he heard footsteps. He raced behind the closest row of lockers and flattened himself against the wall. Someone was turning the corner.

Mr. Garcia, Nathan thought. *He must have forgotten something.* Luckily, the teacher didn't see Nathan, and he disappeared through the door to the classroom. Nathan held his breath. This was better than he'd hoped. He had planned for Mr. Garcia to find the elf the next morning before school started, but now . . .

Ah, the terrifying scream!

Nathan smiled. Best prank ever. He stayed hidden a few more minutes. He'd leave as soon as Mr. Garcia came back out and left. But he didn't. Ten, twenty minutes went by, and the teacher still had not come out.

Nathan started sweating. *Sooner or later,* he thought, *another teacher or grown-up will come walking down the hall. They'll ask what I'm doing, and then . . . I'll be caught. I need to get out of here!*

So without a backward glance, Nathan flew down the hall toward the front door. He ran

all the way home. His ribs were burning by the time he reached the garage. But he didn't care. It was all worth it. Mr. Garcia would never learn who had left the elf, never know who had given him the fright of his life. *Serves him right,* thought Nathan. *No one gives me a C minus.*

The next morning in Mr. Garcia's room, the students got a surprise. Sitting in their teacher's chair was the school principal, Mrs. Holloway.

"Good morning, class," she began. "I have some bad news, I'm afraid. Mr. Garcia will not finish the rest of the year with us."

Nathan's stomach turned to ice and his thoughts started racing. *Did the shock of seeing the spooky elf make Mr. Garcia sick? Was it his heart? Was he in the hospital?*

Nathan glanced nervously around the room. The elf was nowhere in sight. Someone must have thrown it away.

Mrs. Holloway walked to the door, smiling. She turned to the class. "But don't worry," she said cheerfully. "We were lucky enough to find a substitute." Mrs. Holloway opened the door and called, "Won't you please come in, Ms. Selph?"

A merry little woman stepped into the room. Her curly hair was lobster red. She wore an emerald green sweater with a white puffy collar. Her eyes were shiny and hard. Her cheeks were rosy. And her smile was wide as a shark's.

The chill spread from Nathan's stomach to his chest, his neck, his face.

"Children, Ms. Selph will be your new teacher for the rest of the year," said Mrs. Holloway. "Can we all say 'good morning'?"

"Good morning, Ms. Selph," echoed the class.

Ms. Selph beamed at the students. Her smile, if it was possible, grew even wider.

"Wonderful," she said. Her voice sounded bright as a bell. "I'm so glad to be here. I know it must be quite a surprise to have a new teacher in the middle of the year," she went on. "But not all surprises are bad."

Her shiny eyes blinked, and she looked right at Nathan. "Don't you just love surprises?" she asked.

THE PHANTOM ON THE PHONE

Ella received an odd text on her phone one morning from her friend Hayley.

Who's the girl in your pic???

Ella texted back:

What pic????

Hayley sent a pic with her next text.

This selfie u sent. Who's the girl in the background?

Ella looked closely at her phone. The picture was of her, Ella, making a goofy face at the camera. It was taken in Ella's backyard, full of bright sunshine. *I don't remember this*, thought

Ella. In the background, beside the birdfeeder in the middle of the yard, stood a tall, skinny girl.

Ella zoomed in, but the image got fuzzier. It was hard to make out the girl's face, but Ella could tell there was something disturbing about it. She texted Hayley.

Does she have a monkey face?

Hayley replied:

LOL she does!!

It must be a mask, thought Ella. *But who is she?*

Then Hayley sent another photo.

Whats the joke? U just sent this one 2

Ella stared at her phone screen. *What is Hayley talking about?* she wondered. *I didn't send anything.*

The new photo showed the backyard again. Ella was not in the picture this time. The camera shot a view of her back door. The girl was standing there, reaching for the door handle.

Thinking of the back door of their house, which opened directly into the kitchen, Ella shouted from her bedroom. "Mom! Are you in the kitchen?"

Ella didn't get a response. "Mom?" she called again. No reply, but she heard the back door slam shut.

Her phone chirped — Hayley again.

U r 2 2 funny El

Another photo. This showed the hallway leading to Ella's bedroom. The right side of the pic was fuzzy. It looked like a girl's shoulder.

"Mom?"

There was a creak in the hallway. Ella's house was old, and the uncarpeted floors always creaked and groaned whenever someone walked across them.

Chirp. Another pic from Hayley. This photo showed a close-up of Ella's bedroom door from the outside. A shadow that looked like a hand was reaching for the knob.

Ella had had enough. Why was Hayley pulling this prank on her? And why was Hayley sending

her pics that she, Ella, was supposed to be taking? Wouldn't she have already seen those pictures?

Ella tapped Hayley's phone number on her screen and waited. Finally, Hayley came on. "Hey, El, what's up?" she said, brightly.

"Ha, funny, " said Ella. "You know what's up all right."

"What are you talking about?"

"The pictures," said Ella angrily. "Why do you keep texting me and sending me those creepy pictures?"

There was silence from the other end of the line. Then Hayley said, "I haven't been texting you. I'm helping my brother with his homework."

"Then why do you keep sending those —"

"I haven't been sending you anything," said Hayley. Now it was her turn to sound angry. "And I don't even know what pictures you're talking about. Why did you call me up just to yell at me?"

"I'm not yelling at you!" said Ella.

Click! Hayley hung up.

Ella couldn't move. She sat on her bed, warm sunshine spilling across her jeans, and shivered. The knob turned. Slowly, the door pushed open.

"Who's there?" said Ella. The door opened. Her mom stood there, hand on the knob, smiling at her.

"Are you all right?" asked her mom. "You look worried."

Ella gave a little laugh. "I'm fine. I was just texting with Hayley."

"Well, that's good," said her mom. "Because there's a friend here to see you."

"Who?" asked Ella.

"I've never met her before," said her mom. "She said she's in your class."

Ella slowly got up and followed her mother into the kitchen. A cold wave of fear washed over her.

"That's funny," said her mother. "She was right here."

"I have to call Hayley," said Ella. She ran back to her room.

As she flung open the door, she froze. A monkey-headed girl was sitting on her bed.

ABOUT THE AUTHOR

Michael Dahl, the author of the Library of Doom and Troll Hunters series, is an expert on fear. He is afraid of heights (but he still flies). He is afraid of small, enclosed spaces (but his house is crammed with over 3,000 books). He is afraid of ghosts (but that same house is haunted). He hopes that by writing about fear, he will eventually be able to overcome his own. So far it is not working. But he is afraid to stop. He claims that, if he had to, he would travel to Mount Doom in order to toss in a dangerous piece of jewelry. Even though he is afraid of volcanoes. And jewelry.

ABOUT THE ILLUSTRATOR

Xavier Bonet is an illustrator and comic-book artist who resides in Barcelona. Experienced in 2D illustration, he has worked as an animator and a background artist for several different production companies. He aims to create works full of color, texture, and sensation, using both traditional and digital tools. His work in children's literature is inspired by magic and fantasy as well as his passion for the art.

MICHAEL DAHL TELLS ALL

Can you imagine what a mad scientist's laboratory looks like? You've probably seen one in a movie or video game or comic book. The lab is crammed full of odds and ends, like weird electrical equipment, jars full of squishy stuff, animal skeletons, and ancient books with crumbling pages. I sometimes think of my brain as a laboratory. Mine is packed with memories, riddles, and jokes, voices of people I've met, stories from my family, pictures I've seen in books or museums. And when I start thinking of writing a story, I start picking up odd scraps, bits and pieces here and there. Like a mad scientist, I fit them together into a strange new invention. Here's a list of some of the nuts and bolts that helped build the stories in this book.

HALLOWEEN HEAD

Ordinary objects can become frightening when they appear in places you don't expect them. I was looking at my stash of brown paper grocery bags the other day and asked myself, *Could these be scary? They're so harmless and normal.* Then I wondered, *what if you put something into a bag and then it wasn't there?* I was thinking about all this a few weeks before Halloween. One windy October night all the pieces of the story fit together like the bones of a skeleton. My favorite part of the story: the little eyeholes in the bag.

CHALK

I saw a young girl holding a stick of chalk, and I immediately thought it was a bone. (I hope it wasn't!) After a few hours at my computer, I had the first draft of the story.

NIGHT CRAWLERS

The word "night crawler" gives me the creeps. When I heard about a movie that came out with that title, an image flashed through my mind of a human crawling at night through dark, lonely woods. Crawling and crawling. I had to find out where that person came from, so I wrote the story to find out.

THE WORLD'S MOST AWESOME TOOTHPASTE

You've seen those ads on television that promise amazing results from their super cool products. But who are those people who sell them? And who makes that stuff? It could come from anywhere, right? So what if someone, like a well-meaning mother, ordered a product like that for her kids? Things could go terribly wrong.

THE BACK OF THE CLOSET

Ever since I was five years old and dreamed that a steady stream of bears came lumbering out of my closet toward me, I have not cared much for them. They're dark, stuffy, and things can get easily lost inside them. Closets, I mean, not bears. What if something *worse* than a bear was inside a closet?

THE ELF'S LAST TRICK

The elf is real and has been a member of my family's Christmas tradition for many years. It currently resides in my basement. At least, I *think* it's still down there . . .

THE PHANTOM ON THE PHONE

I was brainstorming with my friend Benjamin Bird about the terrifying possibilities surrounding photos on a phone. With some instant phone messaging apps, the pictures disappear after only a few minutes. Ben pointed out that if you saw something bizarre or unusual on one of these pics, you wouldn't always be able to show other people. The evidence could quickly disappear. How would you convince your friends that you were telling the truth about an upsetting photo? You'd be the only one who saw it. And some apps are so easy even a monkey could use them.

GLOSSARY

awesomeness (AW-suhm-nis) — the state of being terrific or joyous

bendable (BEND-uh-buhl) — able to be bent or twisted without breaking

deserve (di-ZURV) — to earn something because of something you have done

designed (di-ZINED) — drew a plan for something that can be made

endless (END-lis) — having no end or seeming to have no end

goose bumps (GOOS buhmps) — bumps that appear on your skin when you are cold or frightened

impression (im-PRESH-uhn) — an idea or feeling based on something you saw, read, or heard

overdrive (OH-vur-drive) — a state of increased activity

prank (PRANGK) — a playful, mischievous trick

startled (STAHR-tuhld) — surprised or frightened

substitute (SUHB-sti-toot) — someone or something acting or used in place of another

tatters (TAT-urss) — parts left torn or hanging

torso (TOR-soh) — the part of the body between the neck and the waist, not including the arms

victim (VIK-tuhm) — a person who is cheated, tricked, hurt, or made to suffer

DISCUSSION QUESTIONS

1. In "The World's Most Awesome Toothpaste," Jared can't stop brushing his teeth, even though he knows it is bad for him. Talk about a time when you kept doing something even though you knew it wouldn't be good for you.

2. Ella and her friend Hayley are sending text messages back and forth in the story "The Phantom on the Phone" when they realize that there's a girl in the pictures that neither of them recognizes. Who do you think the girl is? What do you think she will say or do once she meets Ella?

3. In "The Elf's Last Trick," Nathan's plan to trick his teacher goes farther than he expected. Have you ever tricked or played a prank on someone? Discuss how it turned out.

WRITING PROMPTS

1. I wrote the story "The Back of the Closet" from the point of view of a monster hiding in a closet. Pretend you're the person in the story who opens the door and write the scene from your own point of view.

2. In the story "Chalk," Jordan arrives at his house and finds that his sister Nyla is drawing incredible art, which she says she can do only because a "poor lady" gave her special chalk. Read the story again, and write the scene where Nyla meets the "poor lady."

3. "Night Crawlers" ends when Sean and Jeremy paddle across the lake to escape from people crawling up from underground and chasing them. What do you think might have happened if the boys had stayed on shore? With that in mind, write a different ending to the story.

MICHAEL DAHL'S
REALLY SCARY STORIES